Bakary On Safari

ISBN: 0-9993307-4-8
ISBN 13: 978-0-9993307-4-6

Published in the United States of America by Fye Network.

To the real Bakary, we love you dearly!
May your love for animals continue to grow.
Stay curious and adventurous!

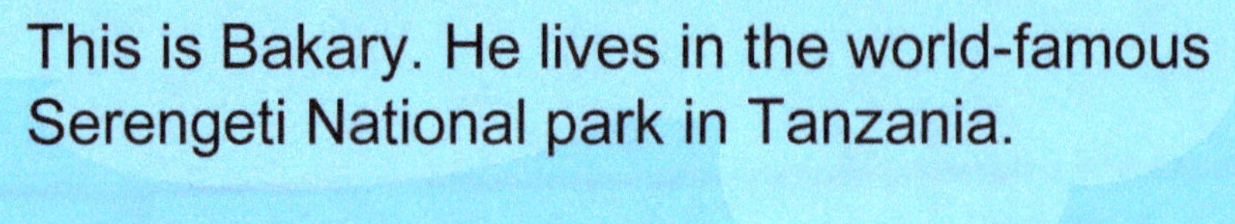

This is Bakary. He lives in the world-famous Serengeti National park in Tanzania.

This is Bakary's dad Juma. He owns a safari tour company and gives exciting tours around the Serengeti.

This is Bakary's mom Nandi. She is a veterinarian and helps animals in the park, especially when they're injured.

Just like his parents Bakary loves animals and the animals love him.

Bakary has three close friends who live in the park too!

His best friend is Blue. Blue is a blue-eared starling that fly's all over the park listening for information. He always has the news of the day.

His other friend is Zuri. Zuri is a wise Elephant. She always has a good folk story to share or a riddle for Bakary, Blue and Flick to solve.

Wherever you see Bakary, he is carrying Flick around his neck. Flick is Bakary's really cool talking camera. He helps Bakary take beautiful photos during their adventures across the park.

Bakary loves to join his dad when the tourists flock to the park to see all the beautiful animals and scenery. And on every adventure the troublesome hyena Tizo is always up to no good.

On sunny days like today, Bakary likes to sit on top of his favorite hill to watch the Zebra's as they go on their daily grazing.

Bakari and his friends are stopped in their tracks when they come across a group of buffalos.

The buffalos were on their usual grazing route but they found the route blocked by a large mud hole.

Tizo the hyena created the mud hole to disrupt the buffalo’s migration

Bakary and his friends help the buffalos build a bridge to cross over the mud hole using some fallen branches.

Bakary was glad to help the buffalos and took some beautiful pictures with Flick as they sat on the hill watching the last of the buffalos cross the bridge.

From a distance Bakary heard his mother calling for him “Bakary, its dinner time, come on inside” said Mama Nandi.

“See you later Zuri and Blue” said Bakary as he took off running with Flick hanging on tight.

“Enjoy your dinner Bakary” screamed Zuri and Blue as they watched him run towards his beautiful cabin home.

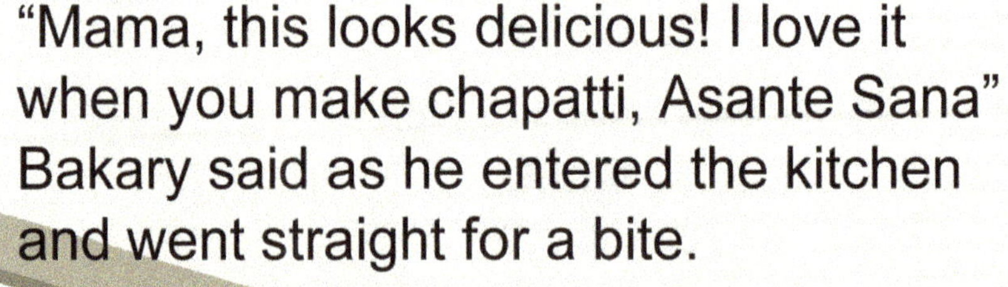

"Mama, this looks delicious! I love it when you make chapatti, Asante Sana" Bakary said as he entered the kitchen and went straight for a bite.

"You are most welcome mpenzi wangu. I love to cook for my favorite boy! But wash your hands first" Mama Nandi said as she finished setting the table.

Just as he finished washing his hands, Papa Juma walks in after finishing his last tour of the day.

Bakary loves dinner time because he gets to hear all about his papa's and mama's day.

They all sat down to enjoy the delicious food and listened to Papa Juma as he shared how the tourist today enjoyed following the great herds of buffalo.

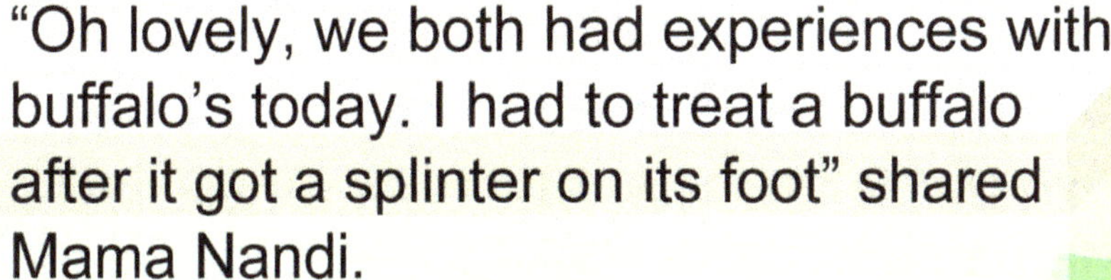

“Oh lovely, we both had experiences with buffalo’s today. I had to treat a buffalo after it got a splinter on its foot” shared Mama Nandi.

“Me too, I had to help some buffalos today!” shared Bakary. “ I love that you love our animals as much as we do” said Mama Nandi with Papa Juma nodding in agreement.

After dinner, Bakary had a nice bath, and it was time for bed.

But of course, Bakary was not at all sleepy and he asked for a bedtime story.

“Only one book tonight not five Bakary” said Mama Nandi as she settled in next to him on the bed.

When they've finished reading, Mama Nandi gives Bakary a kiss and says "I love you my little animal lover! usiku mwema".

And Bakary gives her a kiss back and says “I love you always my favorite animal doctor”.

THE END

www.ingramcontent.com/pod-product-compliance
Lightning Source LLC
Chambersburg PA
CBHW070619310726
48982CB00001B/126
* 9 7 8 0 9 9 9 3 3 0 7 4 6 *